It's Great to Share

Jordan Collins • Stuart Lynch

make believe ideas

"Good morning, class," Miss Clayton said.
"I can see you're all ready for our **field trip**, so let's get going!"

The children cheered.
It wasn't every day they visited
the **petting zoo!**

Before lining up, Sean grabbed his book about goats.
He **couldn't wait** to read about the animals they would be seeing.

On the bus, Ryan and Sean were sitting together.

"Can I see your book?" Ryan asked Sean.

"No," Sean said. "I want to read it myself."

"But I want to read it, too. Can we **share** it?"
Sean **shook his head** and went on reading.

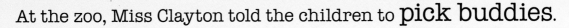

At the zoo, Miss Clayton told the children to **pick buddies**.

"Want to be my buddy?" Sean asked Ryan.

Ryan **shook his head** and **went away**.

Sean was the only student without a buddy.

"Just stay close by, Sean," said Miss Clayton.

Sean nodded, but inside he felt **unhappy** and **confused**.

Later, the children were given hay to feed a goat.

When the bowl got to Sean, he took **all the hay** that was left.

"I didn't get to feed the goat," Abby said to Sean.
"Will you **share** with me?"

Sean shook his head. "No, I got here first," he said.

Next, the class visited the education center to make animal pictures.

Sean **grabbed** the lizard stencil. "Can I use that after you?" Jack asked.
"**No,**" said Sean. He wanted to be the **only one** with a lizard picture.

"You're not very good at sharing," Jack said, and then he left.

Maybe I'm not the best at sharing, Sean thought to himself.

But he didn't mind that. Sharing meant giving up something he wanted.

It was lunchtime.

Sean finished his sandwich and went to find his friends.

They were playing with the cool **wind-up tiger** Ryan had bought at the zoo shop.

"Can I play?" Sean asked.

"No," Ryan said.

ZOO SHOP

Sean folded his arms.
"That's not fair!"
he said.

"You **don't share** with us,"
Abby said, "so why should we
share with you?"

Sean didn't understand. "You're supposed to be my friends," he said.

Sean trudged back to the lunch table, feeling confused.

"Miss Clayton, my friends **won't play with me,**" he said sadly.

"Oh dear! That must feel horrible,"
said Miss Clayton.
"Did your friends say why?"

"They said I **don't share with them**, but why does that matter?"

"Well, if you want people to **share with you,
you have to share with them.**
Would you like it if you shared your football with Ryan,
but he didn't share his markers with you?"

Sean thought hard.

"No," he said, "that wouldn't be fair."

Sean suddenly realized that it **wasn't much fun** to be around someone who **didn't share.**

Sean thought, *You do have to* give up something
if you don't share - your friends.

"Thanks, Miss Clayton," he said.

"You're welcome," Miss Clayton replied, and she pulled something out of her bag.

"I've got some popcorn," she said. "Would you like it?"

"Sure!" Sean said. "Thanks!"

He was about to eat it when he had a thought.

"Miss Clayton, can I go find **my friends?**" he asked.

"Yes, just stay nearby," Miss Clayton replied.

Sean raced over to his friends with the popcorn in his hand.

"I'm sorry I was selfish," he said.
"Do you want to share my popcorn?"

"Yeah," Jack said, grinning. "I love popcorn!"
The friends **shared** the bag.

While Sean ate, he thought about how much fun
it was to **share with friends**.

READING TOGETHER

The Let's Get Along! books have been written for parents, caregivers, and teachers to share with young children who are developing an awareness of their own behavior.

The books are intended to initiate thinking about behavior and empower children to create positive circumstances by managing their actions. Each book can be used to gently promote further discussion around the topic featured.

It's Great to Share is designed to help children realize that sharing not only makes others feel good but also the person who is doing the sharing. Once you have read the story together, go back and talk about any similar experiences the children might have had with sharing and not sharing. Ensure children understand that everyone can be a little thoughtless sometimes and that, like Sean, they can take steps to repair relationships that may have been damaged.

As you read

By asking children questions as you read together, you can help them engage more deeply with the story. While it is important not to ask too many questions, you can try a few simple questions, such as:

- What do you think will happen next?

- Why do you think Sean did that?

- What would you do if you were Sean?

- How does Sean make up for his behavior toward his friends?

Look at the pictures

Talk about the pictures. Are the characters smiling, laughing, frowning, or confused? Do their body positions show how they are feeling? Discuss why the characters might be responding this way. As children build their awareness of how others are reacting to them, they will find it easier to respond in an understanding way.

Questions you can ask after reading

To prompt further exploration of this behavior, you could ask children some of the following questions:

- How do you feel when others share with you? What about when they don't share?

- Can you think of times when it was difficult to share or fun to share?

- Can you think of different ways you can share things with other people?

- When is it a good idea not to share something?
  (For example: with food and drinks; with children who are too young for something; or with people we are not sure we can trust.)